What Do You Love About You?

KAREN LECHELT

BLOOMSBURY

NEW YORK LONDON OXFORD NEW DELHI SYDNEY

First published in the United States of America in December 2016 by Bloomsbury Children's Books
www.bloomsbury.com

Bloomsbury is a registered trademark of Bloomsbury Publishing Plc

For information about permission to reproduce selections from this book, write to Permissions, Bloomsbury Children's Books, 1385 Broadway, New York, New York 10018
Bloomsbury books may be purchased for business or promotional use. For information on bulk purchases please contact Macmillan Corporate and Premium Sales Department at specialmarkets@macmillan.com

Library of Congress Cataloging-in-Publication Data
Names: Lechelt, Karen, author.
Title: What do you love about you? / by Karen Lechelt.
Description: New York : Bloomsbury, 2016.
Summary: Different animals show there is a lot to love about each of us.
Identifiers: LCCN 2015046574
ISBN 978-1-68119-093-8 (hardcover)
Subjects: | CYAC: Self-esteem—Fiction. | Individuality—Fiction. | Animals—Fiction. | BISAC: JUVENILE FICTION/Love & Romance.
| JUVENILE FICTION/Animals/General. | JUVENILE FICTION/Social Issues/Friendship.
Classification: LCC PZ7.1.L393 Wh 2016 | DDC [E]—dc23
LC record available at https://lccn.loc.gov/2015046574

Art created with Photoshop • Typeset in Gyant • Book design by John Candell
Printed in China by Leo Paper Products, Heshan, Guangdong
1 3 5 7 9 10 8 6 4 2

All papers used by Bloomsbury Publishing, Inc., are natural, recyclable products made from wood grown in well-managed forests.
The manufacturing processes conform to the environmental regulations of the country of origin.

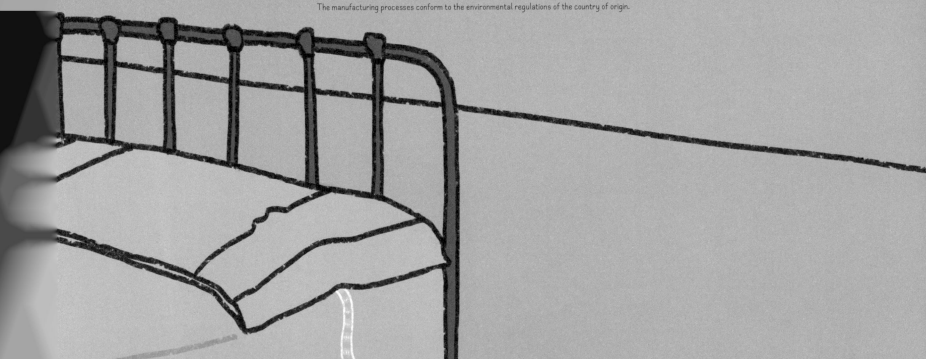

for my moon

What do you love about you?

I love my ears
because your
whispers tickle.

What do you love
about you?

I love my legs because I get
a kick out of you.

What do you love
about you?

I love
my cheeks
because
blowing kisses
is fun!

What
do
you
love
about
you?

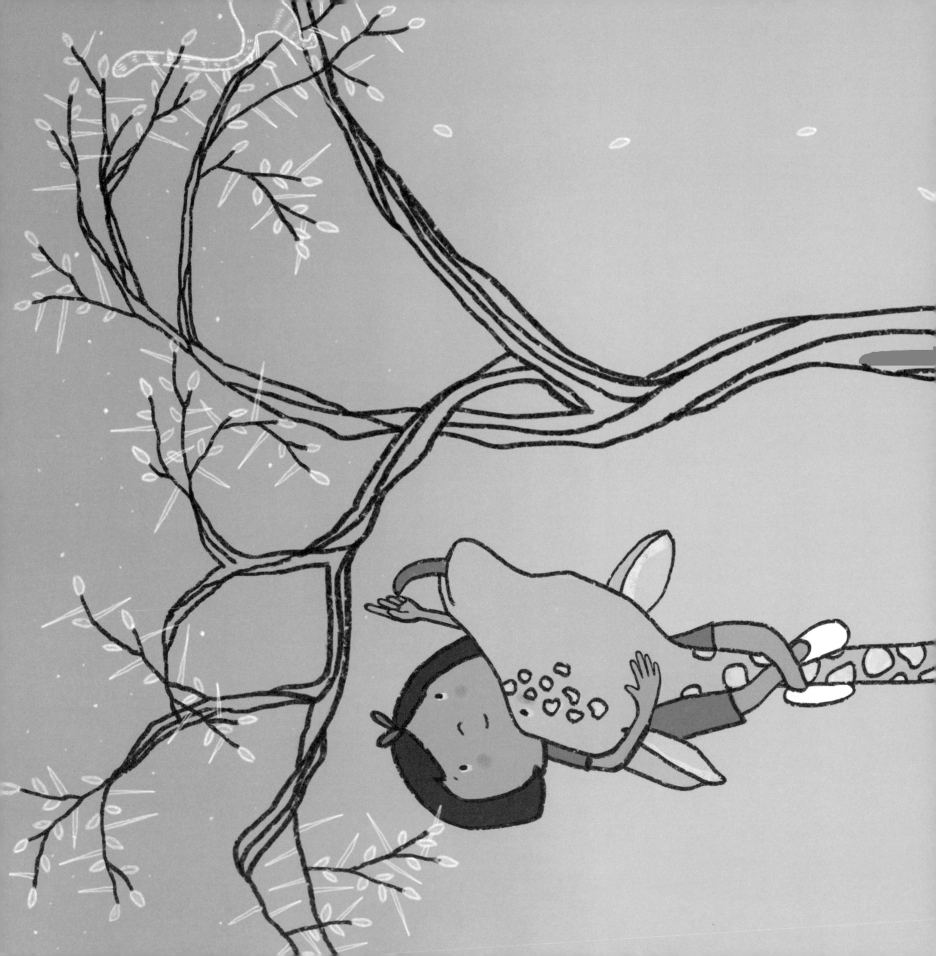

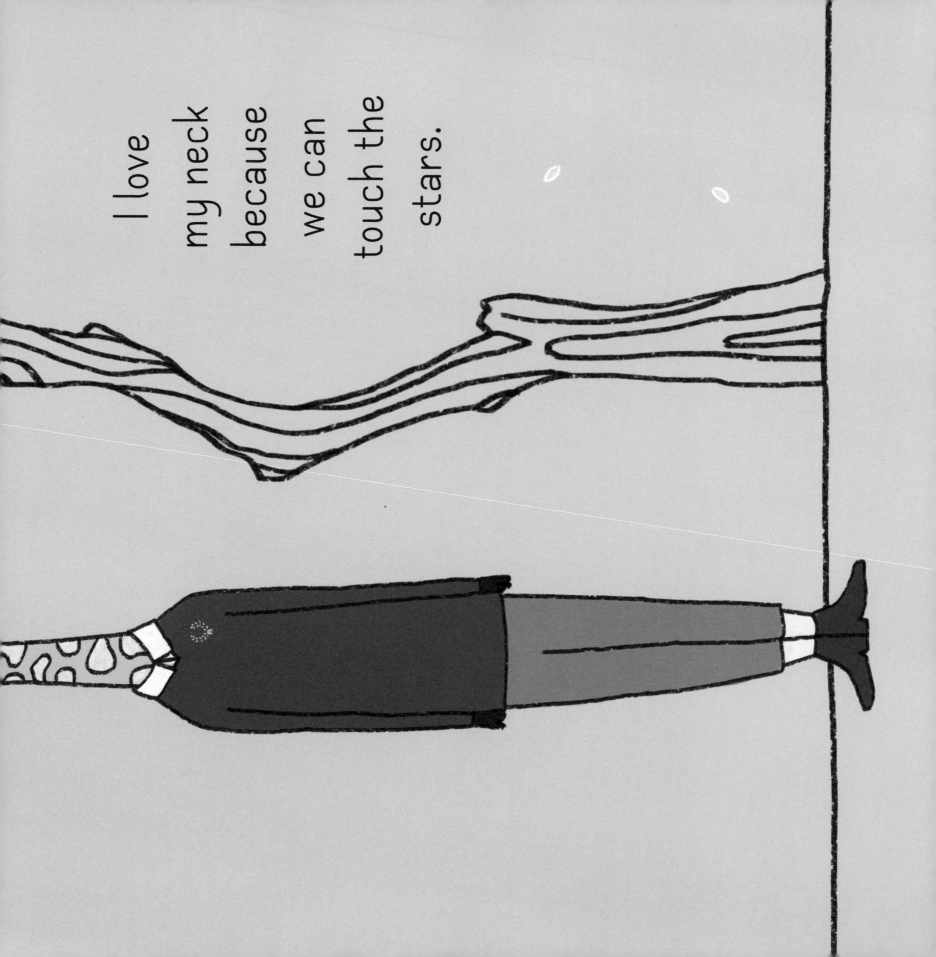

I love
my neck
because
we can
touch the
stars.

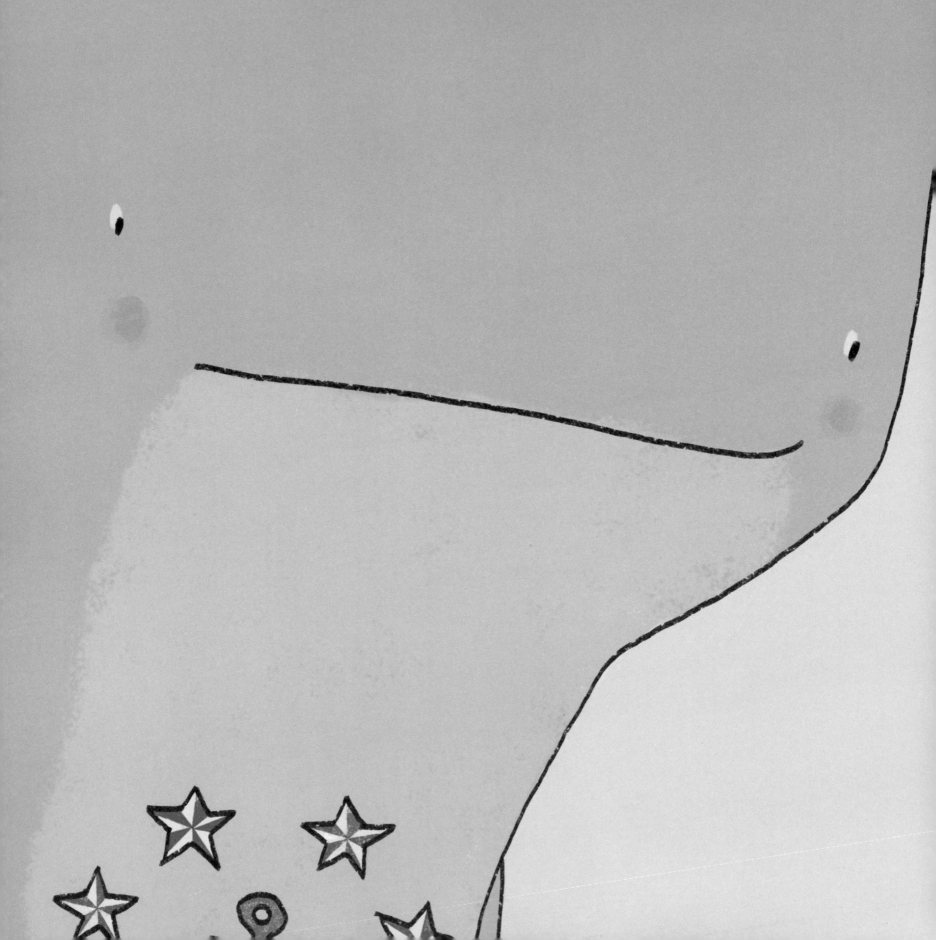

What do you love
about you?

I love my spout because singing in the rain makes me happy.

What do you love about you?

I love my nose because life is sweet.

What do
you love
about you?

I love
my teeth
because I
can change
the world.

What do you love about you?

I love my trunk because
I can swing you to the moon.

What do you love about you?

I love
my antlers
because
without
them
I'd be
lonely.

What do you love
about you?

I love my
tentacles
because
I am a
hugging
machine.

What do I love
about me?

I love my . . . self.